PETER RABBIT
AND HIS FRIENDS
STICKER BOOK

™

From the original and authorized stories
BY BEATRIX POTTER

™

F. WARNE & C°

THE STORY OF THE RABBIT FAMILY

Once upon a time there was a family of rabbits who lived in the woods at the back of Mr. McGregor's garden. They were called Flopsy, Mopsy, Cotton-tail and Peter, and they lived in a sand-bank under a big fir-tree with their mother, Mrs. Josephine Rabbit. She was a widow and earned her living from selling tea and tobacco and knitting rabbit-wool mittens. Mr. Rabbit, their father, had had an unfortunate accident whilst collecting vegetables from Mr. McGregor's garden. He had been caught and put in a pie by Mrs. McGregor.

Flopsy, Mopsy, Cotton-tail and Peter had a favourite cousin who's name was Benjamin Bunny. He was named after his father who was known as Old Mr. Benjamin Bunny. Peter and Benjamin were very naughty little rabbits and, despite Mr. Rabbit's terrible accident, they kept on going into Mr. McGregor's garden to take his vegetables. This was very, very dangerous and on several occasions they nearly had nasty accidents too!

When they grew up, Peter Rabbit had his own nursery garden where he grew flowers and vegetables. Benjamin Bunny married his cousin Flopsy and they had a large family who were known as the 'Flopsy Bunnies'. They had healthy appetites and when there wasn't quite enough food to go round, their Uncle Peter gave them cabbages from his garden. When he had no cabbages to spare, the Flopsy Bunnies raided the rubbish heap outside Mr. McGregor's garden. Once they were caught and almost ended up in a pie like their grandfather. But, thanks to a resourceful friend, the baby rabbits escaped this terrible fate.

The rabbit family tree introduces you to the characters and shows you how they are related to each other, and the tales of Peter Rabbit, Benjamin Bunny and the Flopsy Bunnies tell you about some of their most exciting adventures.

THE RABBIT FAMILY TREE

Mrs. Josephine Rabbit

Old Mr. Benjamin Bunny

Peter   Cotton-tail Mopsy   Flopsy   Benjamin

The Flopsy Bunnies

The Story of Peter Rabbit

Once upon a time there were four
little Rabbits, and their names
were –

Flopsy,
Mopsy,
Cotton-tail,
and Peter.

They lived with their Mother in a sand-
bank, underneath the root of a very big
fir-tree.

'Now, my dears,' said old Mrs. Rabbit
one morning, 'you may go into the
fields or down the lane, but don't go
into Mr. McGregor's garden: your
Father had an accident there; he was
put in a pie by Mrs. McGregor.'

'Now run along, and don't get into
mischief. I am going out.'

Then old Mrs. Rabbit took a basket
and her umbrella, and went through
the wood to the baker's. She bought a
loaf of brown bread and five currant
buns.

Flopsy, Mopsy, and Cotton-tail, who
were good little bunnies, went down
the lane to gather blackberries:

But Peter, who was very naughty,
ran straight away to Mr. McGregor's
garden, and squeezed under the gate!

First he ate some lettuces and some
French beans; and then he ate some
radishes;

And then, feeling rather sick, he
went to look for some parsley.

But round the end of a cucumber
frame, whom should he meet but Mr.
McGregor!

Mr. McGregor was on his hands
and knees planting out young
cabbages,
but he jumped up and ran after
Peter, waving a rake and calling out,
'Stop thief!'

Peter was most dreadfully
frightened; he rushed all over the
garden, for he had forgotten the way
back to the gate.

He lost one of his shoes among the
cabbages, and the other shoe amongst
the potatoes.

After losing them, he ran on four legs and went faster, so that I think he might have got away altogether if he had not unfortunately run into a gooseberry net, and got caught by the large buttons on his jacket. It was a blue jacket with brass buttons, quite new.

Peter gave himself up for lost, and shed big tears; but his sobs were overheard by some friendly sparrows, who flew to him in great excitement, and implored him to exert himself.

Mr. McGregor came up with a sieve, which he intended to pop upon the top of Peter, but Peter wriggled out just in time, leaving his jacket behind him.

And rushed into the tool-shed, and jumped into a can. It would have been a beautiful thing to hide in, if it had not had so much water in it.

Mr. McGregor was quite sure that Peter was somewhere in the tool-shed, perhaps hidden underneath a flower-pot. He began to turn them over carefully, looking under each.

Presently Peter sneezed – 'Kertyschoo!' Mr. McGregor was after him in no time.

And tried to put his foot upon Peter, who jumped out of a window, upsetting three plants. The window was too small for Mr. McGregor, and he was tired of running after Peter. He went back to his work.

Peter sat down to rest; he was out of breath and trembling with fright, and he had not the least idea which way to go. Also he was very damp with sitting in that can.

After a time he began to wander about, going lippity – lippity – not very fast, and looking all round.

He found a door in a wall; but it was locked, and there was no room for a fat little rabbit to squeeze underneath.

An old mouse was running in and out over the stone doorstep, carrying peas and beans to her family in the wood. Peter asked her the way to the gate, but she had such a large pea in her mouth that she could not answer. She only shook her head at him. Peter began to cry.

Then he tried to find his way straight across the garden, but he became more and more puzzled. Presently, he came to a pond where Mr. McGregor filled his water-cans. A white cat was staring at some gold-fish, she sat very, very still, but now and then the tip of her tail twitched as if it were alive. Peter thought it best to go away without speaking to her; he had heard about cats from his cousin, little Benjamin Bunny.

He went back towards the tool-shed, but suddenly, quite close to him, he heard the noise of a hoe — scr-r-ritch, scratch, scratch, scritch. Peter scuttered underneath the bushes. But presently, as nothing happened, he came out, and climbed upon the wheelbarrow and peeped over. The first thing he saw was Mr. McGregor hoeing onions. His back was turned towards Peter, and beyond him was the gate!

Peter got down very quietly off the wheelbarrow, and started running as fast as he could go, along a straight walk behind some black-currant bushes.

Mr. McGregor caught sight of him at the corner, but Peter did not care. He slipped underneath the gate, and was safe at last in the wood outside the garden.

Mr. McGregor hung up the little jacket and the shoes for a scare-crow to frighten the blackbirds.

Peter never stopped running or looked behind him till he got home to the big fir-tree.

He was so tired that he flopped down upon the nice soft sand on the floor of the rabbit-hole and shut his eyes. His mother was busy cooking; she wondered what he had done with his clothes. It was the second little jacket and pair of shoes that Peter had lost in a fortnight!

I am sorry to say that Peter was not very well during the evening.

His mother put him to bed, and made some camomile tea; and she gave a dose of it to Peter!

'One table-spoonful to be taken at bed-time.'

But Flopsy, Mopsy, and Cotton-tail had bread and milk and blackberries for supper.

The Tale of Benjamin Bunny

One morning a little rabbit sat on a bank.

He pricked his ears and listened to the trit-trot, trit-trot of a pony.

A gig was coming along the road; it was driven by Mr. McGregor, and beside him sat Mrs. McGregor in her best bonnet.

As soon as they had passed, little Benjamin Bunny slid down into the road, and set off – with a hop, skip and a jump – to call upon his relations, who lived in the wood at the back of Mr. McGregor's garden.

That wood was full of rabbit holes; and in the neatest sandiest hole of all, lived Benjamin's aunt and his cousins – Flopsy, Mopsy, Cotton-tail and Peter.

Old Mrs. Rabbit was a widow; she earned her living by knitting rabbit-wool mittens and muffetees (I once bought a pair at a bazaar). She also sold herbs, and rosemary tea, and rabbit-tobacco (which is what *we* call lavender).

Little Benjamin did not very much want to see his Aunt.

He came round the back of the fir-tree, and nearly tumbled upon the top of his Cousin Peter.

Peter was sitting by himself. He looked poorly, and was dressed in a red cotton pocket-handkerchief.

'Peter,' – said little Benjamin, in a whisper – 'who has got your clothes?'

Peter replied – 'The scarecrow in Mr. McGregor's garden,' and described how he had been chased about the garden, and had dropped his shoes and coat.

Little Benjamin sat down beside his cousin, and assured him that Mr. McGregor had gone out in a gig, and Mrs. McGregor also; and certainly for the day, because she was wearing her best bonnet.

Peter said that he hoped that it would rain.

At this point, old Mrs. Rabbit's voice was heard inside the rabbit hole, calling – 'Cotton-tail! Cotton-tail! fetch me some more camomile!'

Peter said that he thought he might feel better if he went for a walk.

They went away hand in hand, and got upon the flat top of the wall at the bottom of the wood. From here they looked down on Mr. McGregor's garden. Peter's coat and shoes were plainly to be seen upon the scarecrow, topped with an old tam-o-shanter of Mr. McGregor's.

Little Benjamin said, 'It spoils people's clothes to squeeze under a gate; the proper way to get in, is to climb down a pear tree.'

Peter fell down head first; but it was of no consequence, as the bed below was newly raked and quite soft.

It had been sown with lettuces.

They left a great many odd little foot-marks all over the bed, especially little Benjamin, who was wearing clogs.

Little Benjamin said that the first thing to be done was to get back Peter's clothes, in order that they might be able to use the pocket handkerchief.

They took them off the scarecrow. There had been rain during the night; there was water in the shoes, and the coat was somewhat shrunk.

Benjamin tried on the tam-o-shanter, but it was too big for him.

Then he suggested that they should fill the pocket handkerchief with onions, as a little present for his Aunt.

Peter did not seem to be enjoying himself; he kept hearing noises.

Benjamin, on the contrary, was perfectly at home, and ate a lettuce leaf. He said that he was in the habit of coming to the garden with his father to get lettuces for their Sunday dinner.

(The name of little Benjamin's papa was old Mr. Benjamin Bunny.)

The lettuces certainly were very fine.

Peter did not eat anything; he said he should like to go home. Presently he dropped half the onions.

Little Benjamin said that it was not possible to get back up the pear-tree, with a load of vegetables. He led the way boldly towards the other end of the garden. They went along a little walk on planks, under a sunny red-brick wall.

The mice sat on their door-steps cracking cherry-stones, they winked at Peter Rabbit and little Benjamin Bunny.

Presently Peter let the pocket-handkerchief go again.

They got amongst flower-pots, and frames and tubs; Peter heard noises worse than ever, his eyes were as big as lolly-pops!

He was a step or two in front of his cousin, when he suddenly stopped.

This is what those little rabbits saw round that corner!

Little Benjamin took one look, and then, in half a minute less than no time, he hid himself and Peter and the onions underneath a large basket . . .

The cat got up and stretched herself, and came and sniffed at the basket.

Perhaps she liked the smell of onions!

Anyway, she sat down upon the top of the basket.

She sat there for five hours.

* *

I cannot draw you a picture of Peter and Benjamin underneath the basket, because it was quite dark, and because the smell of the onions was fearful; it made Peter Rabbit and little Benjamin cry.

The sun got round behind the wood, and it was quite late in the afternoon; but still the cat sat on the basket.

At length there was a pitter-patter, pitter-patter, and some bits of mortar fell from the wall above.

The cat looked up and saw old Mr. Benjamin Bunny prancing along the top of the wall of the upper terrace.

He was smoking a pipe of rabbit-tobacco, and had a little switch in his hand.

He was looking for his son.

Old Mr. Bunny had no opinion whatever of cats.

He took a tremendous jump off the top of the wall on to the top of the cat, and cuffed it off the basket, and kicked it into the green-house, scratching off a handful of fur.

The cat was too much surprised to scratch back.

When old Mr. Bunny had driven the cat into the green-house, he locked the door.

Then he came back to the basket and took out his son Benjamin by the ears, and whipped him with the little switch.

Then he took out his nephew Peter.

Then he took out the handkerchief of onions, and marched out of the garden.

When Mr. McGregor returned about half an hour later, he observed several things which perplexed him.

It looked as though some person had been walking all over the garden in a pair of clogs – only the foot-marks were too ridiculously little!

Also he could not understand how the cat could have managed to shut herself up *inside* the green-house, locking the door upon the *outside*.

When Peter got home, his mother forgave him, because she was so glad to see that he had found his shoes and coat. Cotton-tail and Peter folded up the pocket handkerchief, and old Mrs. Rabbit strung up the onions and hung them from the kitchen ceiling, with the bunches of herbs and the rabbit-tobacco.

The Tale of The Flopsy Bunnies

It is said that the effect of eating too much lettuce is 'soporific.'

I have never felt sleepy after eating lettuces; but then *I* am not a rabbit.

They certainly had a very soporific effect upon the Flopsy Bunnies!

When Benjamin Bunny grew up, he married his Cousin Flopsy. They had a large family, and they were very improvident and cheerful.

I do not remember the separate names of their children; they were generally called the 'Flopsy Bunnies.'

As there was not always quite enough to eat, – Benjamin used to borrow cabbages from Flopsy's brother, Peter Rabbit, who kept a nursery garden.

Sometimes Peter Rabbit had no cabbages to spare.

When this happened, the Flopsy Bunnies went across the field to a rubbish heap, in the ditch outside Mr. McGregor's garden.

Mr. McGregor's rubbish heap was a mixture. There were jam pots and paper bags, and mountains of chopped grass from the mowing machine (which always tasted oily), and some rotten vegetable marrows and an old boot or two. One day – oh joy! – there were a quantity of overgrown lettuces, which had 'shot' into flower.

The Flopsy Bunnies simply stuffed lettuces. By degrees, one after another, they were overcome with slumber, and lay down in the mown grass.

Benjamin was not so much overcome as his children. Before going to sleep he was sufficiently wide awake to put a paper bag over his head to keep off the flies.

The little Flopsy Bunnies slept delightfully in the warm sun. From the lawn beyond the garden came the distant clacketty sound of the mowing machine. The blue-bottles buzzed about the wall, and a little old mouse picked over the rubbish among the jam pots.

(I can tell you her name, she was called Thomasina Tittlemouse, a woodmouse with a long tail.)

She rustled across the paper bag, and awakened Benjamin Bunny.

The mouse apologized profusely, and said that she knew Peter Rabbit.

While she and Benjamin were talking, close under the wall, they heard a heavy tread above their heads; and suddenly Mr. McGregor emptied out of a sackful of lawn mowings right upon the top of the sleeping Flopsy Bunnies! Benjamin shrank down under his paper bag. The mouse hid in a jam pot.

The little rabbits smiled sweetly in their sleep under the shower of grass; they did not awake because the lettuces had been so soporific.

They dreamt that their mother Flopsy was tucking them up in a hay bed.

Mr. McGregor looked down after emptying his sack. He saw some funny little brown tips of ears sticking up through the lawn mowings. He stared at them for some time.

Presently a fly settled on one of them and it moved.

Mr. McGregor climbed down on to the rubbish heap.

– 'One, two, three, four! five! six leetle rabbits!' said he as he dropped them into his sack. The Flopsy Bunnies dreamt that their mother was turning them over in bed. They stirred a little in their sleep, but still they did not wake up.

Mr. McGregor tied up the sack and left it on the wall.

He went to put away the mowing machine.

But Mrs. Tittlemouse was a resourceful person. She nibbled a hole in the bottom corner of the sack.

The little rabbits were pulled out and pinched to wake them.

Their parents stuffed the empty sack with three rotten vegetable marrows, an old blacking-brush and two decayed turnips.

While he was gone, Mrs. Flopsy Bunny (who had remained at home) came across the field.

She looked suspiciously at the sack and wondered where everybody was?

Then the mouse came out of her jam pot, and Benjamin took the paper bag off his head, and they told the doleful tale.

Benjamin and Flopsy were in despair, they could not undo the string.

Then they all hid under a bush and watched for Mr. McGregor.

Mr. McGregor came back and picked up the sack, and carried it off.

He carried it hanging down, as if it were rather heavy.

The Flopsy Bunnies followed at a safe distance.

They watched him go into his house.

And then they crept up to the window to listen.

Mr. McGregor threw down the sack on the stone floor in a way that would have been extremely painful to the Flopsy Bunnies, if they had happened to have been inside it.

They could hear him drag his chair on the flags, and chuckle – 'One, two, three, four, five, six leetle rabbits!' said Mr. McGregor.

'Eh? What's that? What have they been spoiling now?' enquired Mrs. McGregor.

'One, two, three, four, five, six leetle fat rabbits!' repeated Mr. McGregor, counting on his fingers – 'one, two, three –'

'Don't you be silly; what do you mean, you silly old man?'

'In the sack! one, two, three, four, five, six!' replied Mr. McGregor.

(The youngest Flopsy Bunny got upon the window-sill.)

Mrs. McGregor took hold of the sack and felt it. She said she could feel six, but they must be *old* rabbits, because they were so hard and all different shapes.

'Not fit to eat; but the skins will do fine to line my old cloak.'

'Line your old cloak?' shouted Mr. McGregor – 'I shall sell them and buy myself baccy!'

'Rabbit tobacco! I shall skin them and cut off their heads.'

Mrs. McGregor untied the sack and put her hand inside.

When she felt the vegetables she became very very angry. She said that Mr. McGregor had 'done it a purpose.'

And Mr. McGregor was very angry too. One of the rotten marrows came flying through the kitchen window, and hit the youngest Flopsy Bunny.

It was rather hurt.

Then Benjamin and Flopsy thought that it was time to go home.

So Mr. McGregor did not get his tobacco, and Mrs. McGregor did not get her rabbit skins.

But next Christmas Thomasina Tittlemouse got a present of enough rabbit-wool to make herself a cloak and a hood, and a handsome muff and a pair of warm mittens.

The Peter Rabbit Crossword Puzzle

This crossword puzzle tells the story of Peter's adventures in Mr. McGregor's garden. You can complete the sentences below and fill in the crossword with the help of the written clues and the picture clues beside each column. We have also filled in some of the letters to make it a bit easier.

When you have finished you can check your answers at the back of the book.

CLUES

1 (down)   Peter squeezes under the _g_ __ _t_ __.
1 (across) In the garden, he __ __ _t_ __ some radishes.
2 (down)   He eats so much that he feels rather __ __ _c_ __.
2 (across) Then suddenly, Mr. <u>M</u> <u>c</u> <u>G</u> __ __ _g_ __ __ appears!

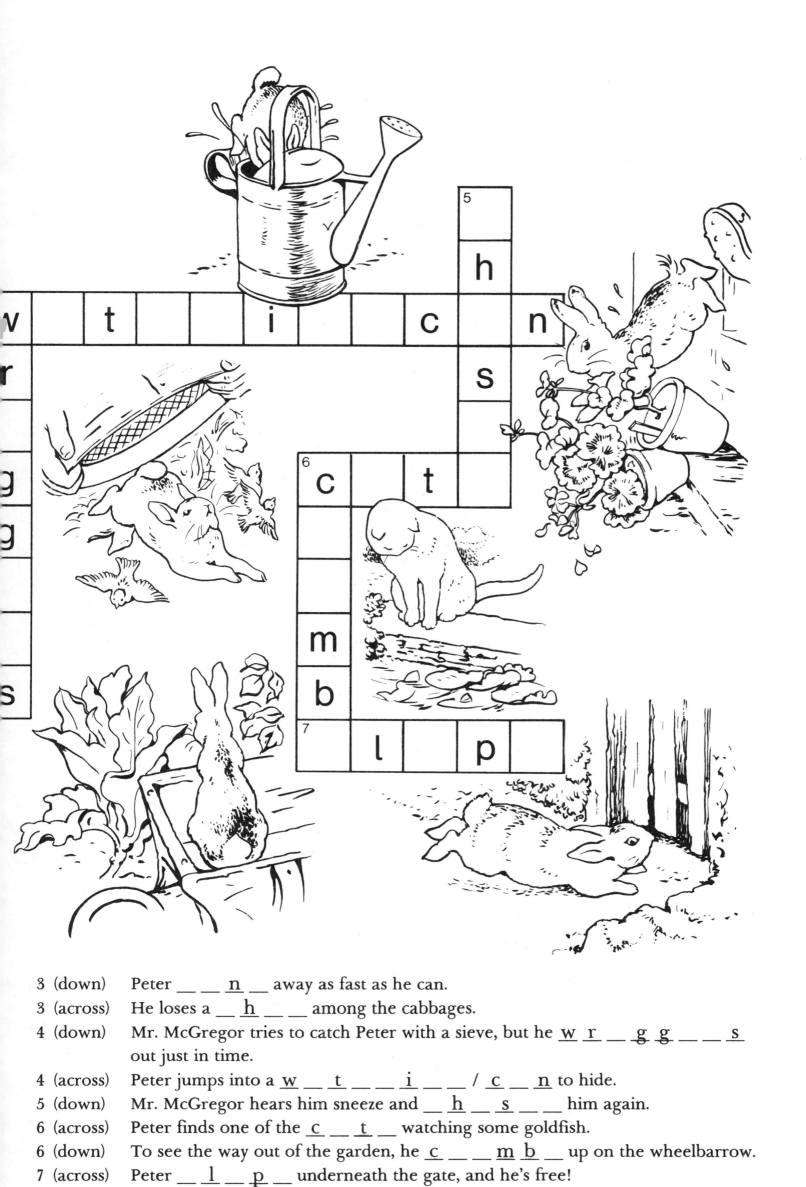

3 (down)   Peter __ __ n __ away as fast as he can.

3 (across)   He loses a __ h __ __ among the cabbages.

4 (down)   Mr. McGregor tries to catch Peter with a sieve, but he w r __ g g __ __ s out just in time.

4 (across)   Peter jumps into a w __ t __ __ i __ __ / c __ n to hide.

5 (down)   Mr. McGregor hears him sneeze and __ h __ s __ __ him again.

6 (across)   Peter finds one of the c __ t __ watching some goldfish.

6 (down)   To see the way out of the garden, he c __ __ m b __ up on the wheelbarrow.

7 (across)   Peter __ l __ p __ underneath the gate, and he's free!

Find the Missing Onions

Peter Rabbit and his cousin Benjamin Bunny have been collecting onions from Mr. McGregor's garden. Peter is startled by a sudden noise and the onions fall out of his pocket-handkerchief. Can you find all 10 of them in the picture and colour them in?

The Flopsy Bunnies' Dot-to-Dot

Three of the Flopsy Bunnies are sitting under Mr. and Mrs. McGregor's kitchen window, listening to them quarrelling.

You can finish the picture by joining up the dots. Be very careful to follow the numbers correctly. When you have done this you can colour the picture in.

Mr. McGregor's Garden Maze

This maze shows Peter Rabbit in Mr. McGregor's garden. There are many different paths through the garden but some are blocked with various obstacles. Can you help Peter to escape to the gate on the other side?

When you have done this, you can fill in the missing letters to complete the word puzzle. This will show you a bird that Peter met in the garden and some things that he lost there as he was trying to escape.

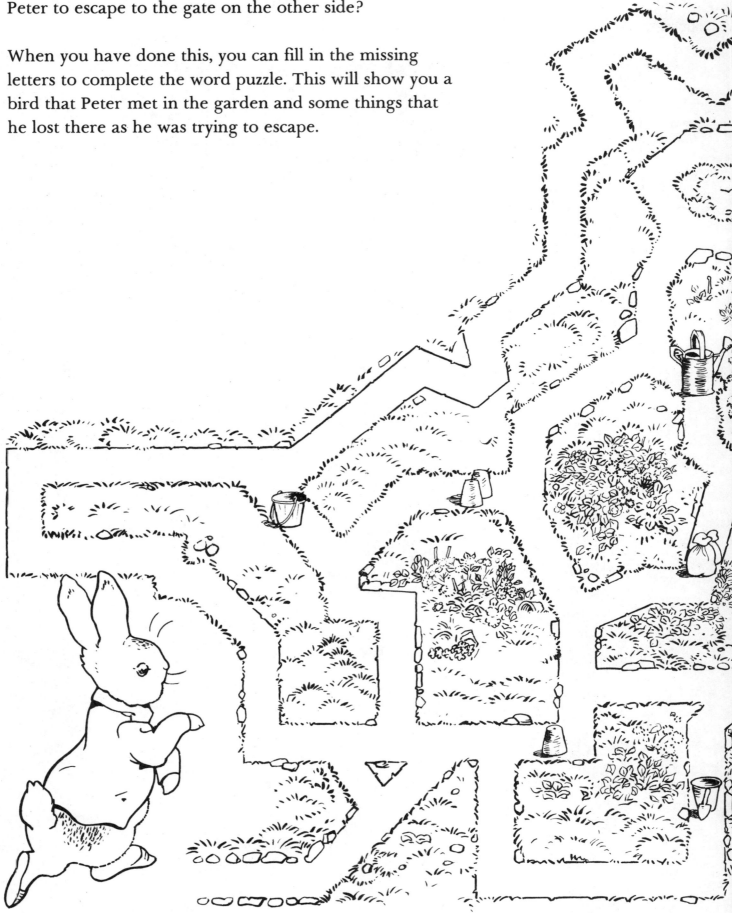

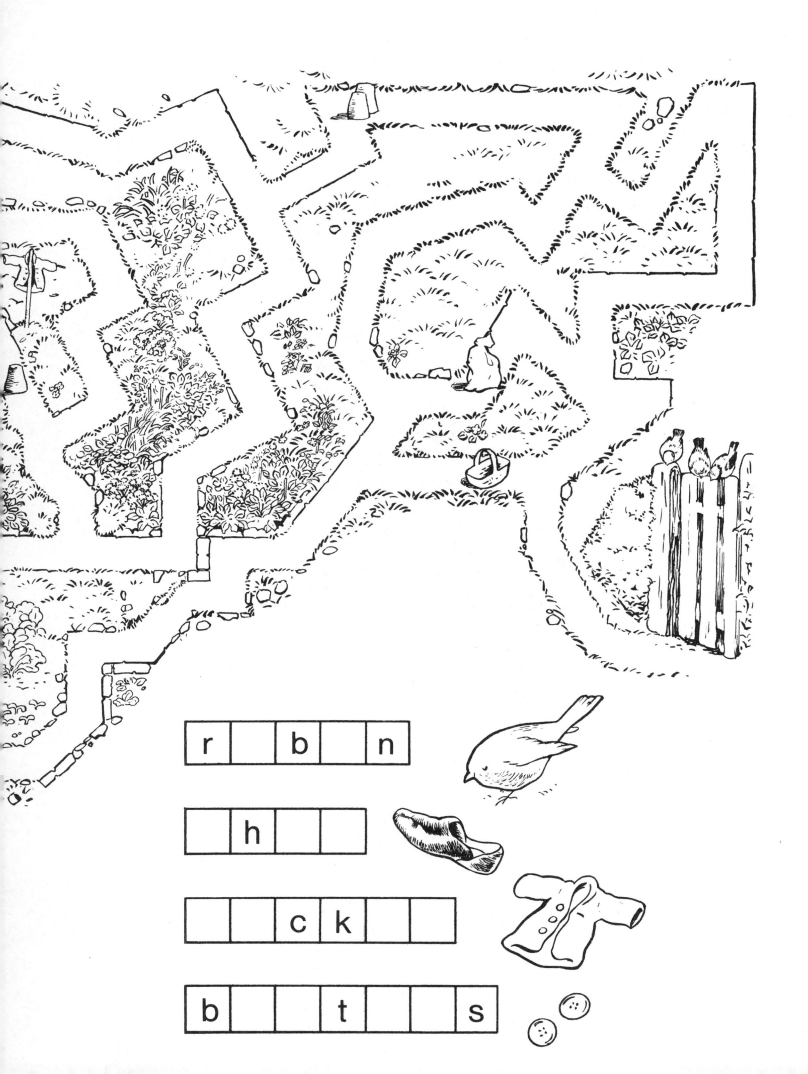

r		b		n

	h		

	c	k		

b		t		s

Answers to the Peter Rabbit Crossword Puzzle

1 (down)   Peter squeezes under the <u>gate</u>.

1 (across)   In the garden, he <u>eats</u> some radishes.

2 (down)   He eats so much that he feels rather <u>sick</u>.

2 (across)   Then suddenly, Mr. <u>McGregor</u> appears!

3 (down)   Peter <u>runs</u> away as fast as he can.

3 (across)   He loses a <u>shoe</u> among the cabbages.

4 (down)   Mr. McGregor tries to catch Peter with a sieve, but he <u>wriggles</u> out just in time.

4 (across)   Peter jumps into a <u>watering can</u> to hide.

5 (down)   Mr. McGregor hears him sneeze and <u>chases</u> him again.

6 (across)   Peter finds one of the <u>cats</u> watching some goldfish.

6 (down)   To see the way out of the garden, he <u>climbs</u> up on the wheelbarrow.

7 (across)   Peter <u>slips</u> underneath the gate, and he's free!

FREDERICK WARNE

Penguin Books Ltd, 27 Wrights Lane, London W8 5TZ (Publishing and Editorial)
and Harmondsworth, Middlesex, England (Distribution and Warehouse)
Viking Penguin Inc., 40 West 23rd Street, New York, New York 10010, U.S.A.
Penguin Books Australia Ltd, Ringwood, Victoria, Australia
Penguin Books Canada Ltd, 2801 John Street, Markham, Ontario, Canada L3R 1B4
Penguin Books (N.Z.) Ltd, 182–190 Wairau Road, Auckland 10, New Zealand

First published 1987

Copyright © Frederick Warne & Co., 1987
Text illustrations by Colin Twinn
Adapted from illustrations by Beatrix Potter from *The Tale of Peter Rabbit, The Tale of Benjamin Bunny, The Tale of The Flopsy Bunnies,*
The Tale of Mrs. Tittlemouse, The Tale of Timmy Tiptoes, The Tale of Pigling Bland and *Appley Dapply's Nursery Rhymes*
Copyright © Frederick Warne & Co., 1902, 1904, 1909, 1910, 1911, 1912, 1917
Universal Copyright Notice:
Cover illustrations from *The Tale of Benjamin Bunny*
Copyright © Frederick Warne & Co., 1904
Copyright in all countries signatory to the Berne Convention
These reproductions copyright © Frederick Warne & Co., 1987
Copyright in all countries signatory to the Berne and Universal Conventions

ISBN 0 7232 3537 6

Printed and bound in Great Britain by Purnell & Sons (Book Production) Limited, Paulton, Bristol